Henry Haynes
and the
Great Escape

Karen Inglis

Illustrations by Damir Kundalić

~WS~

Well Said Press

Published by Well Said Press 2014
83 Castelnau, London, SW13 9RT, England

ISBN: 978-0-9569323-6-5

www.wellsaidpress.com

For Martha – who read this first

1 THE CHATTERING BOOK

As Henry Haynes cocked his head sideways, trying to read the titles on the library book spines, he was sure he could hear a faint noise. Like distant voices. Murmuring. *Chatter* even. Not normal everyday chatter. This was definitely chatter of the most unusual kind – anything *but* normal as far as Henry was concerned. For a second he thought it was coming from the wall behind the bookshelves, but that was impossible as the wall backed onto the street and he was on the first floor.

He swung round. No-one. Only old Mrs Glyn smiling at him from the checkout desk. 'Three more minutes, dear,' she called. Her voice echoed strangely through the gloom.

Henry narrowed his eyes and glanced sideways, left then right, trying to work out where the voices had come from. Then he realised the chatter had stopped. He gave a puzzled frown, shook his head and turned back to the bookshelf where he was surprised to find a book sticking out at a sharp angle in front of him.

Henry cocked his head sideways and read out loud: **'Jeremy James and The Great Escape'**. He grinned broadly, grabbed the book between his chubby fingers and made his way to the desk.

As Henry laid the book down in front of Mrs Glyn, for a split second he thought he heard the murmuring again. And, for just the briefest of moments, he thought it was coming from the book! He darted a look up at the old lady. But she was busy typing at her computer. Click, click, click. The keys danced merrily beneath her fingers as she hummed a soft tune. Henry frowned. Was it possible Mrs Glyn had been muttering to herself just now?

Mrs Glyn stopped, picked up the book and swiped it in front of the scanner. 'Bleep!'

'There you go, dear,' she said, gently, twirling

round on her chair. And now, as Mrs Glyn handed Henry his book, she gave him the strangest of smiles.

At the same time (was Henry imagining this?) her eyes seemed to be *twinkling*. In fact (no, he definitely wasn't imagining it), the twinkle in old Mrs Glyn's eyes that afternoon was quite unlike anything Henry had ever seen before.

'I think you'll enjoy this one,' she said, in a gentle, smiley kind of voice.

'Thanks,' said Henry, wide-eyed. And he stuffed the book into his rucksack and hurried towards the exit.

§

'Supper, Henry!' His mother was calling up the stairs.

'Drat!' said Henry. He'd only just got home and was eager to make a start on The Great Escape. He yanked the book from his rucksack and opened the first page. He pressed his right ear hard against it, and listened. Silence. He shrugged, then put the book on his bedside table and pulled his stopwatch from his shorts pocket. **"Start!"** At the press of the button Henry flung himself towards the door, switched off the light and thundered down the stairs.

Precisely 12.68 seconds later (a new bedroom-to-kitchen-table record) Henry Haynes shovelled his first mouthful of warm mashed potato into his mouth. At precisely the same time, unknown to Henry, the crisp white pages of *'Jeremy James and The Great Escape'* began glimmering, ever so slightly, in the darkness up in his room. Then – just as Henry's fork pierced his first 'Big Dan' fishcake – it started. The words in the book began whispering, the letters on the pages began nudging one another playfully.

Henry Haynes, who was soon downing 'Big Dan' fishcakes and warm mashed potato faster than an Olympic Eating Athlete, had no idea that things were suddenly *happening* inside his book. No indeed. Henry Haynes, whose tummy was fast filling up, hadn't the faintest inkling.

2 FALLING IN

Henry's tea took him exactly three minutes and forty-two seconds to eat. ('What! No pudding?' said his mother in astonishment.)

Back in his bedroom he leaned over and grabbed '*Jeremy James and The Great Escape*' from his bedside table and held it briefly to his ear again. Still silence. He turned to the first page and read:

'Jeremy James, who was ten years old, was badly in need of an adventure. He had been stuck in bed for three weeks with a very nasty dose of the flu.

'Great news!' his mum cried as she burst into the room after the doctor had gone. 'Doctor says you are better. We can all go out – at last! Now, where would you like to go?'

Jeremy thought for about two seconds then said, 'The Zoo.'

'The Zoo it shall be!' replied his mum.

One hour later Mr and Mrs James and their only child, Jeremy, drove off in their car to the Zoo.'

'I hope there are some baddies in this story,' murmured Henry with a frown. He cupped his chin in his hand and read on.

'Poor Jeremy's face dropped when he saw the zoo

queue, which snaked one hundred metres down the road.

'Don't worry!' said his dad with a chuckle. 'We've got a Family Pass!'

The James family passed quickly through the gates, trying hard not to look too smug. The long faces of everyone queuing gazed despairingly after them.

Their first visit was to the gorilla cage.

'Pooh he stinks!' yelled Jeremy, clutching his nose and rolling his eyes. As everyone around him started to laugh, Jeremy cackled loudly then pointed and shouted 'Stink Face!' at the ape.

At this the gorilla took one step forward and eyeballed Jeremy as it chewed on a piece of straw. Jeremy was then sure he heard it grunt, 'Larf like that again, mate an' I'll 'ave yer fer lunch!'

Immediately Jeremy's face drained and he stopped laughing, but then he remembered that the gorilla was separated from him by a handy set of iron bars. 'Let's find the lions!' he yelled, heading off.

Lions were Jeremy's favourite of all.'

'Brilliant! Lions!' breathed Henry, his brown eyes widening. He read on.

'Jeremy and his parents were just walking towards the lions' den and laughing about how smelly the gorilla was, when an announcement came over the loudspeakers:

'This is an emergency announcement! Please walk quietly towards the exit gates. We regret to inform

you that one of our boa constrictors has escaped and is
at this very moment slithering about somewhere in the
grounds.

'Oh, yes, and ..er.. if you have a toy snake from
the zoo shop, to be on the safe side, please place it
carefully on the grass, walk slowly away from it
backwards, and ..er.. avoid using the name 'Brian'.

'Now - no panicking please, ladies and gentlemen.
There are lives at stake here!'

'An escaped *snake*?' said Henry rather loudly.
'*Why* can't it be an escaped lion?' He snorted
indignantly and continued.

'Suddenly there was the most almighty scream
from a lady sitting on the grass a few metres away
from where the James family stood.

'AAHH... it's the snake!! It's got my ankle!'

Jeremy looked across and there, sure enough, was an enormous glistening boa beginning to coil its brown and black trunk-like body around the ankle of a meek-looking lady with dark curly hair.'

Henry's forehead crumpled into a frown.

'*Why* didn't they make it an escaped lion!' he said crossly, thinking how much more bloodthirsty he could have made the story.

Well that, I'm afraid, did it.

You see, things were already afoot inside Henry Haynes's library book.

And at that moment, just as Henry uttered the word 'lion', a loud tearing noise rose up from the book and a black hole appeared across the middle of the page and began spreading up and outwards towards his pillow.

'This is an emergency announcement! Please walk quietly towards the exit gates. We regret to inform you that one of our boa constrictors has escaped and is at this very moment slithering about somewhere in the grounds. ... you ... a toy snake
'Oh, ye... ... e safe side,
from t... ... the grass,
plea'pl... ... ...rds,
wall w... ...rian'.
anc ... and
'N ... ...ere!'
... ...rther
lou ... ...lion?' He
snc

'Su... ... ...ghty
scre ... ...he grass
not ... ...ie Johnson
f... ...re
... ...t my ankle!'
Jerem... ... ...e, sure
enoug... ... ...istening boa
begi...ning to ...n and black
trunk-like body around the ankle of a meek looking woman with dark curly hair...'

Henry's first thought was to run from the room. But curiosity quickly overtook his fear and as he now poked his nose down into the hole he could see a mass of letters whirling about in what looked like a deep dark cooking pot.

His pillow, which should have been underneath the book, seemed to have vanished,

and a soft chattering noise was rising up and out of
the hole.

Henry leaned farther over to get a better look.
As he did so, he felt a force starting to pull him
towards the hole.

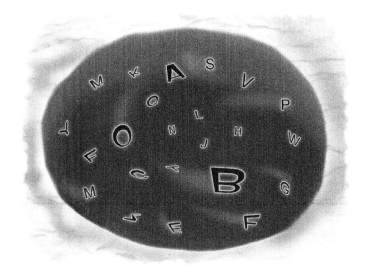

He tried to resist, but couldn't. The hole was
now expanding rapidly – the wider it grew, the
stronger the pull. Within seconds it had consumed
the edges of his book and was eating into his

pillow. And it was then, right out of the blue, that *'Whoosh'* in he fell!

Down into the hole.

Down amongst the mass of chattering letters.

That's right! Henry Haynes, aged ten and three weeks, had tumbled inside his library book!

3 A BUMPY LANDING

As Henry felt himself falling, the chattering of the letters sang out all around. Soon it became so noisy he had to cover his ears with his hands. All around him he could see Bs, Fs, As, Zs, Es, Rs and dozens of other letters whizzing up down, left and right. Most strangely, when he looked up, he could still see his air-balloon lampshade hanging from his bedroom ceiling. Then, as he fell deeper in, and as his bedroom ceiling disappeared behind yet more letters, Henry began to smell fresh air.

Suddenly he saw blue sky. Suddenly he smelled a familiar smell. What was it?

The letters had stopped chattering and were now floating past him, one at a time, as if in space.

After a considerable pause, the letter **B** went bobbing past against the blue-sky background. This was soon followed by an **O**. Next an **A** zigzagged up to him, humming casually, then dodged to his right.

Immediately Henry began to tremble because

he quickly worked out that 'B' 'O' 'A' spelled **BOA**.

Henry was just starting to panic about what he would do if he actually *met* a boa constrictor when 'THUD', down he landed bottom-first on the green zoo grass. When he looked up he saw Brian the boa from his story, still busy coiling himself around the meek lady's ankle.

4 FOLLOW THE SNAKE

'Aaahh…SSSo glad you could make it!'

hissed Brian who immediately loosened his grip
and squinted across at Henry through the sunlight.
The snake quickly uncoiled from the lady's leg and
began slithering in Henry's direction. The meek
lady with the curly hair promptly fainted and was
surrounded by the waiting crowd. No-one seemed
to have noticed Henry's arrival.

Henry froze as the great snake moved in closer.
He was just about to shut his eyes for what he

thought must be the last time on the world when Brian, with his glaring yellow eyes fixed far in the distance, slithered right past him muttering

'Follow me, boy!'

'Where am I? Where are we going?' said Henry, scrambling to his feet. He tried not to gulp.

'You'll sssee sssoon enough,' hissed Brian as Henry hurried helplessly behind.

The signs they passed read 'To the Gorilla Cage', and Henry immediately broke into a cold sweat, trying to decide which was worse; to be crushed to death by a boa or munched by a gorilla with an odour problem. In fact he needn't have worried because ten seconds later they passed right by the ape without stopping.

*'**Morning, Gordon,**'* hissed Brian casually as they passed.

As soon as the gorilla saw Henry, he jumped up and started rattling the side of his cage. *'Ere, you, boy Jeremy!'* he snarled. *'I'll teach you to call me names!'* Henry thought he was going to be sick with the smell, never mind fright, and was glad he had a boa to keep up with. The gorilla obviously thought he was Jeremy from the library book story.

The next sign they passed said: 'To the Lions'. Henry could feel himself starting to sweat again.

Why, oh why, hadn't he kept his big mouth shut about escaping lions? Just look where his whining had landed him! A book with a hole, a gorilla who thought he was Jeremy, and certain death-by-lion.

5 LIONS ON THE LOOSE

As they rounded the next bend the snake suddenly stopped. ***'SSSee over there!'*** he hissed dreamily. Henry followed Brian's gaze towards a distant enclosure. Three lions were lounging in the sun on a rocky mound above a moat, swatting flies with their rope-like tails.

'H-e-a-v-e-n on earth, t-h-a-t'sss where that isss!' sighed Brian.

'Have they had their lunch?' Henry asked in a high voice that didn't sound like his own. His knees had started to tremble.

'*Of coursse,*' hissed Brian with a smile.

Henry heaved a sigh of relief.

But then the snake turned, grinned and winked. '***Ohhh, but they do ssso enjoy their dessert! Now, follow me, boy! Oh, er, and by the way, you can call me Brian you know!***'

'Brian,' squeaked Henry in a whisper.

As Henry and the snake drew closer to the lions' den Henry gathered his senses.

'Now look here, Brian,' he blurted out in his best put-on deep voice, 'you've got the wrong person here! *I'm* not Jeremy. I'm not in this story. *I* don't get eaten by lions! Please, let me go back home!'

The snake stopped abruptly and peered down its nose.

'Get eaten?' he hissed. *'What are you sssaying, dear boy?*

'You, my boy, are here to help usss – not to get eaten! It'sss Revolution Day today!'

He sniffed deeply then lurched forward.

'Now do let'sss get a move on, pleassse.'

'Revolution?' quizzed Henry, panting as he ran to keep up. 'What are you talking about?'

'Revolution! Re-houssing! A new dawn!' sang Brian.

'Re-housing?'

Henry still hadn't the faintest idea what Brian

was talking about, but at least felt grateful he wasn't going to end up in a lion's lunch box.

Soon they reached the solid iron gate that marked the entrance to the lions' den.

Nearby, the crowds pressed their noses on the glass looking in, seemingly unaware of Henry and the snake.

'Now, boy, ssstand back!' hissed Brian.

Henry stepped back just as Brian began to snake his body up into the air. At about three metres high, and almost fully uncoiled, he began humming, then gyrating like a belly dancer while making extremely rude gulping sounds between the hums.

After a few seconds Henry spotted a large round lump travelling up inside Brian's body towards his head.

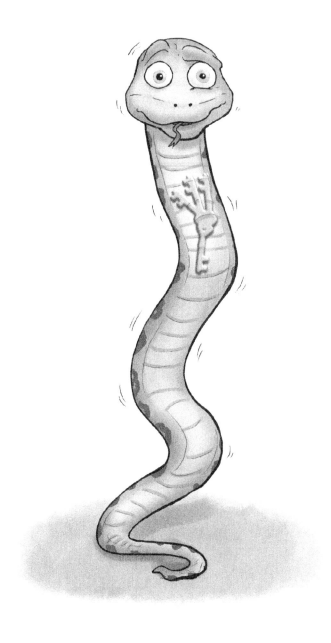

Brian continued humming and gyrating until the lump had almost reached his mouth. Then he let out the most almighty burp and jettisoned an enormous bunch of keys onto the ground – right in front of Henry!

'Oooh! That'sss better!' hissed Brian with a wide-mouthed grin. *'I've been wantin' to do that for agesss!'*

Henry stared at the saliva-covered keys in

horror then slowly looked up at Brian.

Brian raised his eyebrows knowingly then bounced a glance from the keys, to Henry, to the gate-lock.

'No way!' shouted Henry, jumping back a pace. 'If you think I'm going to let those lions out you've got *another* think coming! They'll attack people!'

'Tut-tut,' said Brian shaking his head. ***'But of courssse you're going to let them out, dear boy! You see, it'sss all part of the plan!'*** He grinned again like a wide-mouthed frog.

'But they'll kill people!' cried Henry. 'They'll eat us all for lunch!'

Brian slithered backwards, then squinted down his nose.

'Don't be ssso ssstupid!' he hissed wearily. ***'Why would the finest pride of lions in***

London waste their appetites on humansss when they can have the bessst sssirloin sssteak thisss side of Hampssstead from their own keepers?!'

The snake's glaring yellow eyes were now level with Henry's, his ghastly slithering tongue tickling Henry's right cheek.

'Now then, boy, LET 'EM OUT! Cos you ain't going home 'til you do!'

Henry had no choice. With wobbling knees and a quivering hand he picked up the warm saliva-covered keys and slowly placed the one marked 'L'

in the lock. As he turned the key to the left he felt a sudden jolt. Then, with a groan and a creak, the great iron doors began to swing open.

The crowds screamed and scattered.

The lions jumped up.

And Henry tiptoed behind the gates.

6 GORDON'S ESCAPE PLAN

'Long live The Revolution!' roared the first lion as it lumbered out through the great iron gates. (The zoo visitors were fleeing in all directions.)

'Thanks, Brian! It's all yours,' came a second growl from the lion behind.

After about a minute, when the screams of the crowds had died away, Henry stepped from behind the vast iron gate to see three yellow lions' tails bobbing up and down in a distant cloud of dust, heading towards the zoo exit. The crowds were still

scattering, and Brian the boa was nowhere to be
seen.

'What now?' thought Henry looking all around.
All he wanted was to get back to his bedroom and
the proper story. 'The lions are out,' he said to
himself. 'Surely Brian will let me go back now?'

At that moment a low humming noise started
up beyond the gates to the lions' den.

Henry peered cautiously in and quickly
spotted Brian draped across a rock with his tail

dangling in the moat.

'Fancy a ssswim?' hissed Brian, slithering down across the rock and into the stream. *'The water'sss really cool, man! And there's ooohh ssso much ssspace compared with my sssilly glass tank!'*

With the lions out of the way Henry was feeling braver. He marched into the den and sat down on a rock. 'Now look here, Brian,' he said sharply, 'I've done what you've asked. I've let out the lions now. So *please*, how do I get home?'

'Patience! Patience!' hissed Brian from the stream. He dived under the water then slithered back up onto the bank. *'Our day's work is not done yet, boy!'*

Henry's stomach turned a slow somersault as his heart dropped towards his shoes.

'Yesss, yesss!' continued Brian merrily.

'You sssee, the giraffesss and the zebrasss are in on our little plan. Oh, and, er, Gordon, of course…'

The snake coughed politely, trying to avoid Henry's piercing stare.

'D..Did you say *G..Gordon?'* stuttered Henry. His heart was now pounding.

'Yes.. Gordon…you know, Gordon the..er..Gorilla.' Brian pretended to busy himself rearranging his coils. *'You may have noticed him earlier? We passed right by him on the way here.'*

All of a sudden the snake looked up, his eyes glowing with admiration.

'Gordon is our hero – he masterminded the whole Revolution you know!'

Henry shuddered. 'No way! Not Gordon! I'll do the others, but I'm *not* letting that gorilla out. He's marked me for his lunch, I know he has! He thinks I'm that boy Jeremy in my library book who called him stink face!'

Brian shook his head impatiently. **'Tut-tut, my boy! Now, I know Gordon getsss people confused from time to time – you know, like when old George Sm–'** The snake paused and stared into the distance. *'Well, perhaps I won't trouble you with that story.... but, yes, really Gordon's as nice as pie, Briany promissses!'*

Henry clutched his stomach and started shaking his head. 'Anyway,' he shouted, 'if this is a revolution, where are the guns then, eh? EH?'

'There aren't any gunsssssilly! Thiss is a Re-housing Revolution!' hissed Brian.

'A *what*?!' cried Henry in despair, trying hard to lower his voice, but failing. 'I haven't the foggiest idea what you're talking about!'

'Quessstionsss, only quesstionsss!' snapped the snake. He thrust the tip of his tail in the direction of the mound. *'Why don't you go and ssstand up there and take a look out, boy! That's where you'll find your answer!'*

Henry shook his head and sighed. He walked over to the mound, climbed wearily up and stood on the highest point.

As he looked out across the grounds of the zoo to the enormous park outside he could just make out the silhouettes of three lions lounging under a tree.

The last of the walkers, picnickers and footballers, along with the people who had been queuing for the zoo, were fleeing over the horizon.

Henry took in a deep breath and gave a puzzled frown – then all of a sudden raised his eyebrows. 'This Revolution isn't to do with fighting,' he whispered to himself. 'It's about better homes for the animals!'

7 DEAL, NO DEAL

'Ssso, how do you like my new pad?' hissed Brian as Henry returned back down the slope. *'Heapsss better than that tiny tank!'*

Brian scratched his cheek with his tail and lifted his chin importantly. *'We did a deal you sssee. Me and the other sssnakes in here. Lionsss, giraffesss and zebrasss out to the people's park.'*

He paused. *'Oh, er, and Gordon'sss opted for Bear Mountain – you know where the* bears live...'

'And the bears?' asked Henry with a gulp.

Brian tossed a weary glance towards the clouds. *'Ohh, sssilly sissy bears! They want to ssstay where they are, don't they? They're just like all the other animals they are – too ssscared to join the Revolution!*

'Mind you,' he hissed, peering cross-eyed down his nose, *'I don't sssuppose they'll last long there, what with Gordon'sss...well, you know, ...washing problem!'*

At the mention of Gordon, Henry started to panic again. He scrabbled madly in his head for ideas. Gordon thought he was Jeremy from his library book, of that he was sure. And it was Jeremy who'd called the gorilla 'stink face'. If Gordon got anywhere near him he'd be pummelled to the ground and crunched to an agonising death!

'Okay, here's my side of the deal,' said Henry

desperately, trickles of sweat tickling his brow. 'I'll

let out the giraffes and zebras. I'll even throw in the elephants if they change their minds and want to join in, *and* fetch your other snake friends for you. But I'm *not* releasing Gordon!'

'No deal!' snapped Brian.

His cool leathery nose was suddenly pressed hard against Henry's, his yellow eyes glaring like fog lamps once more.

'Gordon the gorilla masterminded thisss plan and he'll be none too pleasssed if he don't get to benefit! Now you had better help get 'im out of his cage, matey, cos you're not leaving this ssstory til you do!'

Henry sat down on a log beside the stream and put his head between his knees. This story was way out of control, and he had to find a way out. How could he release Gordon without putting his own life in danger? He stared miserably at his grubby kneecaps and prayed for a miracle.

8 HENRY'S ESCAPE PLAN

After about ten minutes of thinking Henry jumped up. 'I've got it!' he shouted triumphantly.

Brian, who was dozing in the sun on the rocks, jerked so suddenly he almost shed his skin.

When Henry told him his secret plan the snake grinned widely. **'Bessst of luck, Little Geniusss!'** he hissed merrily. **'Now, come along, boy, the Revolution has ssstarted! Let'sss put your little plan to work....! And once they're all out I'll sshow you how to get home.'**

Henry and Brian immediately headed off towards the zebra pen. When they had got only about 20 metres down the path a zookeeper appeared around the corner. Brian quickly slithered behind a bush, whisking Henry in with the end of his tail.

'Brian! Brian! Here Brian, boy! It's Percy Wercy! Your favourite Keep Weeper! Come to daddy, Brian, boy!' sang the zookeeper.

'Ssstupid oaf! Thinksss I'm his pet dog!'
scoffed Brian. Luckily Percy passed by without
spotting them.

Henry and Brian snuck out again. As they
approached the zebra pen, the animals' eyes filled
with glee. A dozen zebras scuffed the ground
impatiently with their front hooves as they
crowded at the gate chanting, '**Ma**sai **Ma**ra **h**ere
we come!'

'Come on, little fella!' one snorted, its striped
ears pricking hard forward as he eyed the keys
eagerly. 'Attaboy!'

Henry chose the key marked 'Z' and placed it
in the lock. The moment the gates flung open the
whole herd of zebras thundered out, almost
flattening Henry and Brian as they passed.

Brian peered after them through the clouds of dust. **'*There'sss gratitude for you,*'** he hissed angrily. The zebras galloped towards the exit.

Thanks to their tall necks, the giraffes were already eyeing up their corner of the park when Brian and Henry arrived.

'So keynd,' they murmured politely as Henry struggled to reach the lock. The tallest of them, seeing that Henry was having trouble opening the gate, lowered her great neck and nudged her nose against the bars.

'Meynd your heads!' she said regally as the tall gate swung open. The herd of giraffes delicately picked a path past Henry and Brian and went sedately on their way.

'Okay,' said Henry. He pulled his stopwatch from his pocket as they turned to head for the gorilla's cage. 'Now for *your* half of the deal before we put my plan into action... Exactly *how* do I get home once I've set up Gordon to escape?'

'Well, er, it'sss quite sssimple, really!' hissed Brian with a coy grin. **'You just, er, ssstand where you first landed, look straight up – and, er, jump!'**

'Is that it?' said Henry in disbelief. It was so simple he suddenly felt rather foolish.

'That'sss it!' hissed Brian smugly as he gazed up at the clouds. But then he glanced sideways at Henry, narrowing his eyes. *'Oh, but don't go gettin' any funny ideas, matey. Cos if you try to essscape before releasing Gordon, Briany promissses the trick won't work!'*

9 GORILLA CHARGE!

Gordon looked meaner than ever as they approached the cage. Henry, who could feel trickles of cold sweat running down his spine, had placed his blue jumper on the grass in exactly the spot he had landed earlier when he fell through the book. Using his stopwatch he had worked out that it would take him exactly fifteen seconds to get to it from the gorilla's gate. Now, as he fumbled with the keys, he glanced back over his shoulder to check the direction he'd need to run in to escape.

A terrible stench filled the air as they drew close to Gordon's cage.

'Afternoon, Gordon,' spluttered Brian, waving the tip of his tail in front of his nose. Henry thought he might be sick again, but managed to swallow hard instead. Gordon, meanwhile, licked his lips and stared at Henry as he grasped the iron bars with his two hairy hands.

'The Revolution isss well underway,' hissed Brian between coughs, *'and I am pleasssed to tell you that thisss young man is about to sssecure your releassse!'*

Gordon's black beady eyes were glued to Henry who, with trembling hands, was fumbling with the key marked 'G'. 'G' for Gorilla. 'G' for Gordon. 'G' for 'Get you for laughing'.

'Th.. This is your k-key,' Henry stammered.

Gordon let go of the bars and glared at the key.

'B..But you mustn't put it in th..the lock until I have c..counted to twenty. The lock's on a sp..special t-timer.' He lifted his stopwatch to make sure Gordon had understood. 'If you o..open it t..t.too soon, the zoo alarm will s..sound.'

Gordon frowned, scratched his head, then grunted and nodded.

Henry, with his arm shaking violently, tossed the keys through the bars as far away from the gate lock as he could manage – whereupon Gordon (who was nobody's fool) immediately dived backwards, grabbed them and hurled himself at the gate.

Henry, who was already counting, turned and fled in the direction of his jumper on the lawn.

'One, two, three, ...' the key was rattling in the lock.

'Four, five,' the lock was turning.

'Six, seven, eight...' a gate was creaking.

'Nine, ten ...' a chest was beating.

'Eleven, twelve, thirteen....'(unlucky for some) Gordon was charging! 'Fourteen'...Henry looked up...only sky...

He looked down... 'Fifteen!' The jumper! But,

oh no! A gorilla's breath on his neck!

Henry looked up and jumped, just managing to grab his jumper as he went. A whirl of letters and Henry Haynes shooting up through the air, his blue jumper covered in grass cuttings trailing in his hand – and somewhere in the distance above what looked like his bedroom light.

Down below Gordon the gorilla charged on past, not a thought in the world for Henry Haynes.

No indeed. Gordon the gorilla's thoughts and dreams were – and always had been – fixed firmly on the distant peaks of his new home on Bear Mountain.

10 THE END

Squidge. Henry landed back on his bed, face down in his pillow, his heart thumping. Slowly he lifted his head. His library book lay open at the last page beside him, not a sign of a hole anywhere.

Henry thought for a moment and looked all around. Then he felt the sharp stab of his stopwatch against his chest. He wrenched it from under his sweaty body. The timer had stopped at 15 seconds.

Henry half smiled. Then, feeling more than a

little wary about falling inside his book again,

grabbed the bedhead with his right hand and the

book with his left – then through squinted eyes

read the last page.

'Jeremy James stood outside his house while the

reporters for the national newspapers took hundreds

of photographs. He had been the hero of the day. He

had beaten off the snake, saved the woman and,

quite remarkably, ushered everyone out of the zoo to safety. It certainly had been a day to remember!

The newspapers were full of the animals' escape the next day. 'All Change At London Zoo,' 'Mystery Boy Masterminds Zoo Plot' 'Zoo Animals Take Park By Force' 'Zoo Keepers Control Park Lions with Sirloin Steak!'

As for the mystery boy who had helped the animals escape, he was never seen again.'

The End

'Henry! What's all that grass doing on your bed?' Henry's mother stood in the doorway, hands on hips. She sniffed deeply. 'And what on *earth* is that disgusting smell? Have you had a dead animal in here?' Henry cleared his throat and jumped off his bed.

'Gorilla socks!' he blurted out with a crimson grin, then darted past her into the hall.

'Gorilla socks?'

The following morning, when Henry passed the book back over the counter to Mrs Glyn, she gave him the widest of smiles for a little old lady.

'Nothing like a good book to take you into another world,' she murmured, her small eyes twinkling. Then she twirled on her seat and danced her fingers across the keyboards. Click, click, click. Click, click, click.

'I'll see you again very soon, dear,' she said in a strange, smiley sort of voice without looking up.

And as Henry turned to leave she started, very gently, to hum.

THE (REAL) END

ABOUT THE AUTHOR

Karen Inglis lives in Barnes, London, England. She has two sons who inspired her to write when they were younger. She also writes for business, but has much more fun making up stories!

Karen's other books include:

Eeek! The Runaway Alien
The Secret Lake
Ferdinand Fox's Big Sleep

You can read the first two chapters of Eeek! at the end of this book ☺

PLEASE WRITE A REVIEW OF HENRY HAYNES!

If you enjoyed Henry Haynes and The Great Escape, please ask an adult to help you leave a review on your chosen online bookstore's website.

You can also leave a comment on Karen's website at **kareninglisauthor.com** – Karen usually replies!

Eeek! The Runaway Alien (7-10 yrs)

Charlie Spruit can't believe his luck when he opens his door to an alien one morning. Who is he? Why has he come? Charlie soon discovers that this alien has run away from space to Earth to be with him because he's soccer mad and the World Cup is on...!

Charlie hides Eeek! in his bedroom where he sleeps on the ceiling – and only tells his best friend, Jake.

All is going surprisingly well until slimy sci-fi mad Sid Spiker, who lives out the back, spots Eeek! through his telescope...

Read the first two chapters of Eeek! at the end of this book!

The Secret Lake (8-11 yrs)

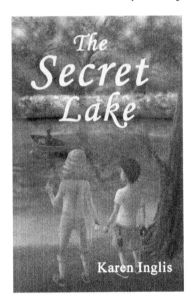

When Stella and her younger brother, Tom, move to their new London home they become mystified by the disappearances of Harry, their elderly neighbour's small dog. Where does he go? And why does he keep reappearing wet-through?

Their quest to solve the riddle over the summer holidays leads to a boat buried under a grassy mound, and a tunnel that takes them to a secret lake. Soon they discover that they have travelled back in time to their home and its gardens 100 years earlier where they meet the children living there...

Search online or visit kareninglisauthor.com

Ferdinand Fox's Big Sleep (3-6yrs)

'Ferdinand Fox curled up in the sun,
as the church of St Mary struck quarter past one.
His tummy was full, he was ready for sleep,
and closing his eyes he began to count sheep.'

A delightful rhyming story about a sleeping fox who is dreaming about the food he loves.

Available as a colour picture book and a separate colouring book. Also as an interactive iPad book app with drag and drop word/picture learning activities.

Search 'Ferdinand Fox' online or in the App Store or visit kareninglisauthor.com

Turn the next page

to read the first two chapters of Eeek!

Eeek!

The runaway alien

KAREN INGLIS

One

It was a fairly typical Saturday morning in our house. Dad was in the garden emptying out the shed (again!). Mum had gone to the gym for her early morning workout. Rory (my four-year-old brother) was on the sofa wearing Dad's snorkel and mask watching his favourite underwater scene in 'Finding Nemo'. I was scoring goals against the kitchen wall in front of an imaginary crowd of 50,000.

That's when the doorbell rang.

'I'll get it!' I shouted. I don't know why I shouted, because I knew that neither Dad nor Rory could hear me. As I rushed down the hall to open the front door I tried to guess which of the following it would be:

- Little Joe Williams from next door asking for his football back (yet again!)
- Someone selling tea towels
- Our postman with a parcel
- The National Lottery man to say we'd won (dream on!)

or

- Mum, hot and sweaty after the gym, having forgotten her key as usual.

In fact it was none of these. Standing at our door that Saturday morning was, I'm not kidding you, an *alien!*

Now, most people would jump out of their skins at the sight on their doorstep of a bald-headed fluorescent green monster with pale blue smoke wafting from its tiny semicircular ears.

But there was something about this alien that touched my heart. Whether it was his large slow-blinking pink- red eyes, his snub nose, his friendly smile, or simply the fact that he was exactly my height, I cannot tell you, but for some reason I just stood there and gawped at him in wonder.

My gawping, and the alien's blinking and smiling, carried on for a good thirty seconds. It was as if I had met a long lost friend and here we were bonding again. But then I nearly jumped out of my skin as an eerie wheezing and rasping noise floated up from behind my right shoulder.

The alien suddenly stopped blinking and

pulled such a terrified face as he stared beyond me I was convinced that an enemy being from the far side of Mercury must have zapped down into my house to do battle with him.

I swung round in fear for my life – to find Rory, complete with snorkel and mask, staring wide-eyed through his steamed-up visor at our visitor.

The alien couldn't handle the sight of Rory. I think it was the batman outfit that finished him off. Without warning he emitted a strange high-pitched echoing sound, then turned and fled out through our gate and off down the road.

'You idiot, Rory!' I shouted. Rory wheezed through his snorkel, then shrugged his shoulders and held up both hands as if to say, 'What did I do?' Then he disappeared back to his 'Finding Nemo' DVD, whisking his cape behind him like a matador with attitude.

'Well,' I thought to myself, 'I've got two choices here. Either I close the door and pretend this never happened, *or* I race down the road to see if I can find the alien and bring him back.' No prizes for guessing which of these two options I picked.

By the time I got to the gate my fluorescent green friend had almost reached the end of our road.

'Come back!' I called in a feeble voice, knowing he wouldn't hear me.

Just at that moment an almighty roar filled the morning sky. I looked up to see the Red Arrows streak out through the white-grey clouds, and cut a cool formation right over the top of the houses at the end of the road. Awesome! When I glanced to the end of the road again, the alien had stopped and was jumping up and down in a frenzy, pointing at the planes.

'Poor soul!' I said to myself. 'Probably thinks it's his spaceship come to rescue him.' It would take more than a puff of blue ear-smoke to get him a ride on one of those! And they definitely wouldn't be taking him home – to the government laboratories more likely!

As their last echo faded across the sky the alien, who had calmed down, didn't, as I thought he would, shoot off around the corner.

Instead he stood there gazing dreamily into the sky, as if he'd just seen Father Christmas and his reindeers, or a few stray angels.

'An alien trance!' I thought as I started walking towards him. At that moment (had he heard my thoughts?) he switched his gaze out of the sky and down the road towards me. Immediately he started waving vigorously. As I approached I could see a broad grin on his moon-shaped face. He seemed to have found his long-lost soul mate again.

'That was the Red Arrows!' I declared with a smile. The alien nodded enthusiastically. 'Did you think they might be your spaceship?' He took a step back a pace and frowned indignantly, as if I'd just said something really dumb. 'So, you speak English?' I faltered, glimpsing his flat, long-toed feet. He pulled a stiff upside-down smile, then gestured as if adjusting an invisible shower control. By this, I think he meant, 'A little.'

'Where do you come from?' I asked, my eyes following his trails of blue smoke upwards.

'Eeek!' screeched the alien in a strange echo, pointing to the sky.

'Of course!' I said smiling. 'I know all about the planets – got a poster in my room, and lots of books. D'you want to come and see? You could show me your home!' I could barely believe my luck when the alien shrugged his shoulders and smiled shyly, as if to say, 'Why not?'

Two

Dad was still in the shed and, judging by the thumps I could hear through the living room wall, Rory was practising diving into the ocean from the sofa. (Either that, or – another of his favourite games – playing Batman leaping from the Empire State Building to catch a baddy.) Mum was still out.

With the coast clear, and, as you might imagine, more than a little excited, I took my alien friend straight up the stairs to my bedroom.

As I opened the door my enormous map of the universe confronted us, hanging directly above my bed, on the opposite side of the room.

I realised at this point it was probably my interest in space (so often mocked by others) that had singled me out for this special visit from an extraterrestrial being. Suddenly I felt privileged. Proud beyond words. Thinking of what my friends were probably doing at this precise moment, I also felt extremely smug.

'Here it is!' I cried confidently, scrambling onto my bed and diving towards the map. 'Now, where are you from?'

No 'Eeek' in reply. No already familiar pant of cool breath behind me. I looked around. To my horror the alien had vanished! Only thin air hovered in my doorway.

'Friend...where are you?' My heart beat furiously. Could I have imagined all this? Just then, to my delight, a puff of blue smoke rose from the foot of my bed, whereupon the alien stood up grinning from ear to ear – holding out my football boots!

'How do you do that?' I gasped, staring at the edges of his mouth. (I swear they *really were* touching his ears!) But my friend wasn't listening. Instead he was fiddling with the laces of the boots, echoing a low hum. Still ignoring me, he sat down on my bed and started putting my boots on. I, meanwhile, began eagerly pointing at my map of the universe quoting the names of the planets, which had moons and how many, and trying to guess which outreach my friend might have come from.

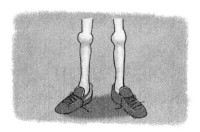

My boots seemed to fit him perfectly, though did look pretty stupid on the end of a pair of knobbly kneed, spindly fluorescent green legs!

'Eeek', as I decided to call him, was now wandering around my room showing more interest in my football posters than any of my space stuff. He even tossed my Stargazer telescope aside in favour of my Northbridge United scarf, which he slung around his neck as he continued to rifle through the mess on my desk. Finally I gave up my tour of the universe and scrambled off my bed. Eeek by now was sitting on the floor thumbing through the pages of my World Cup Sticker Book. When he reached the England team he suddenly stopped and his pale pink eyes filled with tears. Then a pear-shaped drop of water rolled down over his glowing green cheek and landed 'Splat!' right on Joe Carraber's head.

'Hey! Be careful with that!' I lunged forward. Immediately I regretted my outburst, for as I now clutched the book to my chest I could see more and more tears welling in my friend's eyes and, within moments, Eeek was rolling around on the carpet in a near puddle of water, sobbing with a strange echo.

'Look, Eeek, what is it?' I said with a sigh. This alien thing wasn't turning out to be half the fun I'd hoped. Let's face it, what self-respecting 11-year-old wants to spend their Saturday morning with a *crying* alien?

Eeek slowly gathered himself together and wiped away his remaining tears. He then gestured for the book, which I handed over – not without trepidation.

Eeek placed the book on the carpet and eagerly

pointed at the sticker of Northbridge United and England striker, Steve Mitchell.

'Steve Mitchell!' I said with a smile. Eeek nodded enthusiastically. 'Great player!' I added. Eeek clapped his hands. Now we were getting somewhere. 'Hang on? You *know* about Steve Mitchell?' I was talking to *an alien* after all!

Eeek confronted me with another of his indignant frowns.

'Nasty ankle injury,' I muttered vacantly. 'I hope he's okay for England-Brazil on Friday!'

To my horror, Eeek's eyes immediately began glistening again. 'Oh no, Eeek, please! No more crying!' I now had my sanity to think of – not to mention my sodden carpet.

I was glad of my outburst, despite his tears, because Eeek suddenly pulled himself together, jumped up and started practising air kicks in front of my mirror.

'So!' I said. 'You know about the World Cup and

the England Football Team! What else do you know about?'

Eeek gave a knowing wink, then climbed onto the middle of my bed and crossed his spindly legs. A glazed look came over his eyes as he now pointed at his tummy and started rubbing it as he hummed in a high pitch. 'Oh dear, you're hungry!' I said, now wondering what aliens ate for lunch.

Eeek shook his head impatiently then pointed to his tummy again as if to say, 'Look!'

I stared hard at the spot where his belly button should have been, but wasn't. Next thing a rectangle began drawing itself into his translucent green skin. I gasped in horror. *Oh my God! You're a Teletubbie, aren't you? I'm on "You've Been Framed!" aren't I?'* How would I ever live this one down!

Eeek instantly raised his pale pink eyes to the ceiling, then tossed me a cool glance as if to say, 'Boy you really *are* dumb!' He then pointed impatiently at the rectangle in his tummy, which by now was opening like a sideways cat flap.

As the door into Eeek's tummy opened wider, so too did my mouth.

By the time Eeek started reaching *inside* his tummy, I swear, my bottom jaw was all but on the duvet where I sat opposite him.

'What on *earth* are you doing?' I shrieked, fully expecting a blood-soaked intestine to flop out at any moment. (My mum's face on seeing a blood-soaked duvet, along with me and an alien on it, wasn't far from my mind either.)

Eeek echoed a chuckle, and carried on smiling and shaking his head knowingly as his frail green arm reached deeper and deeper inside his tummy.

I was now waiting for his hand to appear out the other side of his back, like a scene from a late night horror film, but it somehow didn't.

'Eeeeeek!' he finally squealed, as though he'd found what he'd been looking for.

My friendly green alien then yanked his hand out and dropped a small purple glowing case onto my bed.

It looked a bit like a little lunch box. The

small door in his tummy conveniently closed itself and disappeared.

I hope you enjoyed the start of Eeek!

You can order *Eeek! The Runaway Alien*

from any bookshop or online.

Happy reading!

Karen

Find out more about Karen and her books at

kareninglisauthor.com